I am the
MOUNTAIN
MOUSE

Gianna Marino

Viking

THE FOOD STORY

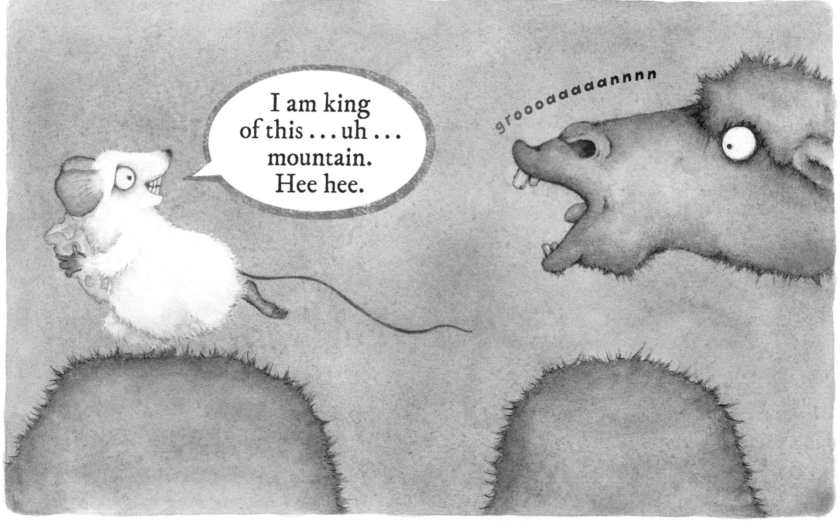

THE POOL STORY

THE COCONUT STORY

THE(RE IS NO) END.

◆——◆——◆

For my team: Tracy, Nancy, Denise, and Deborah.
(Don't worry, none of you is the Mountain Mouse!)

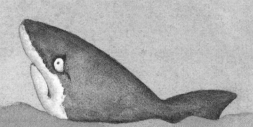

VIKING
Penguin Young Readers Group
An imprint of Penguin Random House LLC
375 Hudson Street, New York, New York 10014

First published in the United States of America by Viking,
an imprint of Penguin Random House LLC, 2016

LIBRARY OF CONGRESS CATALOGING-IN-PUBLICATION DATA IS AVAILABLE
ISBN: 978-0-451-46955-7

Manufactured in China   Set in IM FELL DW Pica PRO   Book design by Nancy Brennan
The illustrations in this book were rendered in gouache and pencil on Fabriano Artistico paper.

1 3 5 7 9 10 8 6 4 2